D0792532

Acclaim for Panio Gianopoulos's *A Familiar Beast*

"Elegant, erudite and witty, this extremely well-observed and surprisingly suspenseful story offers more insights into love and human relationships than most authors manage in works three times as long."

Adam Langer, author of *Crossing California* and *The Thieves of Manhattan*

"Impressively taut and meticulously drawn. As we follow Marcus from reckoning to something like re-demption, Gianopoulous' wisdom and humanity light up this darkly comic, bittersweet journey. Here is a gifted writer in full control of his craft—and impact. *A Familiar Beast* is a perfectly-executed shot through the heart."

Jean Nathan, author of *The Secret Life of the Lonely Doll: The Search for Dare Wright*

"*A Familiar Beast* is superb. Always engaging and often provocative, it follows the gut-tightening travails of a man hollowed by his own infidelities. With elegant prose, unforgettable scenes and Philip Roth-like psychological insights, Panio Gianopoulos's debut novella marks the arrival of a bright and gifted writer."

Jim Lynch, author of *Truth Like the Sun* and *The Highest Tide*

A FAMILIAR BEAST

PANIO GIANOPOULOS

NOUVELLA

2012

A FAMILIAR BEAST

Copyright Panio Gianopoulos 2012

A Nouvella book / published 2012

Design by Daniel D'Arcy

For information go to:
nouvellabooks.com

Printed in the United States of America.

For Molly

A Familiar Beast

"It is a familiar beast to man, and signifies love."
William Shakespeare, *The Merry Wives of Windsor*

Sharon got the Harrisons, the Paulsons, the Davids, and the Martins. She got Genevieve and Jonathan Rich as well as Jonathan's kid sister Willow who, visiting to help with the new baby, judged Marcus's behavior with the pitiless morality of a single woman in her early twenties for whom the many disappointments, compromises, and banal deceptions of a real marriage are as unimaginable as the atmospheric convolutions of the moons of Saturn. After some uncertainty, Sharon secured the Rosses—despite Ted having been one of Marcus's college house-mates in the mid-90s—and though she lost the Galens, Marcus lost them too, so she was willing to let them go.

Of all the friends they had shared as a couple over the years, only Alice Viles was willing to entertain Marcus, but Alice's brother had gone to prison for insider trading seven months earlier and so she was obligated, Marcus reasoned, to carry on about second chances and forgive-ness. She didn't actually like him—a realization Marcus had one day when he stopped by Alice's house to take her up on the open lunch invitation she had extended at the organic supermarket. "Well hello there!" she announced, and in the courteous wrinkle of her voice he heard the disapproval and embarrassment that haunted every interaction these days. Recently disgraced, Marcus found it hard not to catch a secret note of disdain in people's voices, an inevitable, humiliating discovery; wherever he turned, people leaked their derision like potted plants overfilled by amateur gardeners. It was the reason that Marcus had begun to spend more and more time online lately, the reason that he would agree to fly to North Carolina to visit a friend he had not seen in fifteen years and, when there, the reason he would consider, for the first time in his life, tramping out into the wilderness with a gun to kill anything that crossed his path.

Marcus had met Edgar at Pembleton, a small, second-tier New England prep school that included a handful of academically gifted local children as a kind of rueful apology to the community for inflicting upon it two hundred and fifty disorderly rich kids. Though they dabbled with minor gestures of defiance, overall Marcus and Edgar bowed to the influence of their middle-class backgrounds; they were the offspring of families that stressed industry, seriousness, and generational aspiration, and in their mutual concession to obedience they formed a workable friendship. It was a relationship based more on demographic similitude than any innate enthusiasm, however, and after Pembleton ended and each boy went his way, on to college and careers and cities, neither made much of an effort to stay in touch. If it weren't for the encroaching ubiquity of social networking websites, ravenous algorithms that ran on nostalgia and misplaced curiosity, Marcus doubted that they would ever have spoken again. But the world had changed. As had they, Marcus thought, when an unfamiliar man in his mid-thirties, calling Marcus's name, climbed out of a pickup truck in front of baggage claim.

Edgar had lost much of his dark hair; it receded from his temples in a widow's peak and this alteration, combined with the thickening of his once petite nose and the strange, adult bigness of his face in general, rendered him momentarily unrecognizable. He was at once both the boy and not the boy that Marcus remembered, and consequently Marcus felt warring sensations of affection and timidity.

"You must be freezing!" Edgar said, and clubbed Marcus's thin, scalloped shoulder. "Where's your suitcase? We'll throw it in the back."

"Just this," Marcus said, raising his carry-on bag.

"Great!" Edgar announced with cheerful senselessness. He motioned for Marcus to climb into the cab of the truck. It was a massive vehicle, brawny and burnished, with a bolted sideboard to step on while mounting and dismounting. Marcus placed his bag between them on the seat and discreetly brought his palms close to the heating vents. They eased onto Airport Boulevard.

"If you're hungry, say the word. We can stop on the way," Edgar said.

"I'm not hungry."

Marcus observed Edgar take the exit for I-40 East without much interest. Ordinarily, he liked to watch where he was going at all times, compulsively tracking both the route and the direction. Sharon used to tease him that he if he ever had an affair, it would be with the woman who voiced his GPS.

They drove for twenty minutes, discussing the particulars of Marcus's flight from San Jose with a pleasant lack of commitment. When they moved on to the hoary state of air travel in general, Edgar perked up. "Last month, American charged me fifty bucks for an aisle seat! The company paid for it, but the principle of the thing…" he said, and turned onto a side road. A mile and a half later, Edgar steered the truck through a wrought-iron gate that led to two dozen freshly developed houses. Marcus explained that they were all custom, though they were easy to confuse, bearing the resemblance of handsome siblings. Edgar pulled into the driveway of the second-to-last house and switched off the ignition.

"Here we are."

"That's a lot of house," Marcus said, in a tone somewhere between admiration and despondency.

"When I bought it I didn't think I'd be living in it alone."

Marcus climbed out of the truck. He slung his bag over his shoulder while the garage door screamed at him. Edgar ducked inside, brushing past a blue hatchback wedged in tight among cans of plaster, primer, and house paint. Marcus followed behind him, turning his body ninety degrees and scooting sideways to get by the vehicle. As he passed the passenger side, Marcus glanced through the window and noticed that the seat was missing.

"What happened to your car?" he said.

Edgar stared at the space for a second, frowning slightly. "Nothing."

He crouched beside a stack of fifty-pound pallets of corn arranged like overlapping scales. "Hey. Can you carry one of these for me? I'd do it myself but I torqued my back yesterday."

"Where do you need it?"

"The yard. I'll show you where."

Marcus squatted and, scooping up the wide flat bag of feed, he straightened his legs. It wasn't too heavy but it was awkwardly shaped, and Marcus took clumsy steps, his toes turned out for balance and his weight rolled back on his heels. Edgar directed him outside to the yard. It was a long walk to the back of the property. Marcus felt his forearms beginning to tire from the strange grip and he tried to move faster, but the new pace only made it harder to control; the bag shifted against him as he ran, thrashing in his arms like a child demanding to be set down. When he reached the fence, Edgar gestured for Marcus to drop it anywhere. It landed with a deadened thump on the grass. Marcus bent over at the waist and took quick broken breaths.

"I shouldn't give them the whole thing," Edgar said. "Already they've been going through a hundred pounds of this stuff a week. But I figure, with a guest in the house…" He reached up to his belt and slid a folded knife out from its sheath. He offered it to Marcus.

After a moment of hesitation, Marcus took the knife. The rosewood handle was warm and smooth in his palm. He unfolded the blade with a curl of his thumb, feeling the shift in balance, the new extended danger. It was a longer blade than he had expected, pale and serrated, featuring a curve as discreet and elegant as the line of a woman's neck as she arches to show you her indifference.

Marcus kneeled and slit the pallet open. A trickle of dried corn kernels spilled out along the ruptured centerline. He prodded the pallet with the toe of his sneaker, nudging out the contents. "Not like that," Edgar said, motioning for the knife. He took it back and, dropping to one knee, plunged the blade into the corner of the pallet and dragged it across the diagonal. He repeated the cut on the other side. Then he stood and drove the steel toe of his boot into the pallet hard enough to make the vivisected brown body hop.

Minutes later the deer arrived to investigate the gift. Marcus saw them through the glass windows of the dining room, five ghostly shapes coming out of the woods, gently blurring across the dark landscape. He stopped listening to Edgar, in the middle of the tour, and waited to see what the animals would do. They glanced over toward the bright house, intuitively sensing a connection to the creatures inside—or perhaps, Marcus amended, operating simply and consistently out of fear. After a moment, whatever unspoken indicator of safety was communicated and as one they bent their slim auburn necks and began to eat the corn.

"…for all the meals I don't cook," Marcus heard Edgar say, gesturing to the formidable kitchen, stocked with an eight-burner, restaurant-quality gas stove, a prep station with its own sink, and a giddy abundance of granite. The ceiling stood nearly fifteen feet high, and just below it, impossible to reach without a ladder and tremendous resolve, nested a series of little glowing wooden boxes. Within each box rested a vase or glass bowl. Catching Marcus's gaze, Edgar said, "That's the thing about women. They do strange shit like stick a bowl in a box and shine a light on it. Things you just would never think to do."

Marcus showered and slipped on a clean t-shirt. He wore the same jeans he'd worn on the flight; they were the only pants he had brought, and when he held them up to his face he detected a hazy, sweet chemical odor, as if a flight attendant had sprayed his legs with benzene or ozone or some other carcinogen while Marcus negotiated sleep. Then he went downstairs to meet Edgar, who was standing in the pantry, eating Fig Newtons out of the package. It was almost nine o'clock, Edgar explained, and most of the restaurants would be closed now. "It's all families around here." But he knew a bar where they served burgers.

"That sounds great," Marcus said, trying to marshal enthusiasm, leading with the expression of a desired sentiment and hoping that the sensation might obediently follow. It was a strategy that he had used for most of his life, and it had failed him innumerable times. He didn't know what it was that tied him to it, what held him fast to this magical idea—even now, after all the pain it had caused recently—that a feeling could be pre-arranged, ordered in advance and then calmly anticipated. One day, surely, it would arrive, like a phone call from a long-absent lover, confiding I miss you, where are you, come home, please, come home.

Except for a handful of times in high school when they had toddled around the woods in big nervous groups, sipping lukewarm vodka and passing out among the wet ferns, Marcus had never gotten drunk with Edgar, and so he didn't know what to expect when they arrived at the converted firehouse and Edgar swiftly downed a pitcher of beer. To Marcus, who had wedged himself into the end of the pen-scarred wooden booth the way a newborn nestles into the corner of his crib at night, trying to forget that he is dreadfully exposed to life and all its harms, Edgar was a startling eruption of garrulousness and vitality.

"I wasn't even supposed to be in on the deal," Edgar said, "but I made a phone call to a buddy of mine at RFS. I was just taking his temperature, nothing formal. He jumped at it, said he wanted in, so I took that back to Mike and Jonathan and suddenly I was point person for the financing. So when it came time to figure out who was going to run this thing, whatever this thing was becoming, I took Mike aside and said, 'What about Steve Gelson?' And Mike says, 'Absolutely not. Jonathan will hate him. Gelson steals the air out of a room. We don't need that.' So the next day, I call up Steve Gelson. I tell him what we're putting together, by the end of the call he says to me, 'I'm in.' So I go to Mike and I say, 'Good news. Steve Gelson's in,' and Mike says, 'What?

I told you no Steve Gelson.' 'Yeah I know,' I say, 'but just have Jonathan meet with him. He'll love him. Trust me.' So Jonathan meets him later that week and Mike calls me and says 'Jonathan fucking hated him.'"

Shaking his head, he refilled both their glasses with amber faux-German micro-brew. "What about you? You had a thing right? I saw it on your page. Some kind of stadium. You were building a stadium."

"It didn't work out," Marcus said.

"What happened?"

"It was a long time ago. Year and a half."

"You were building a stadium though, right?"

"I wanted to. But nothing got built."

"What happened?"

"A lot of little things went wrong. Then a big thing went wrong."

Marcus dug his thumbnail into a pocket of shredded pulp along the rear corner of the table. He rolled it into a white ball and flicked it away.

"There's always another deal," Edgar said.

"I'm not much of a deal-maker," Marcus said.

"You just have to stick with it. It's a game of last man standing."

The corner of Marcus's mouth curled upward with bitterness. No belief seemed as false to him now as the belief that persistence always wins out in the end. If it weren't for persistence, he would have seen the stadium's failure coming earlier. Rather than disregard the signs— and there had been many—he would have confronted and responded to them. Had he abandoned the project within the first six months, rather than lingering on for two years of mounting debt and desperation, he would never have agreed to accept the job that his wife, at great personal expense, had made available to him. And though the job was destined to be a disaster, when he had tried to articulate the certainty of this outcome to Sharon, she had dismissed his objection. He had been certain about the stadium, too, hadn't he? Maybe it was time to listen to *her* about what would succeed. Here was the rare—maybe the only—opportunity to get his career back on track, and she wasn't going to let him throw it away because, childishly, he didn't like the idea of working for her father. But he would be thirty-two years old and surrounded by twenty-two year olds, he argued. He would be performing drainage and spill prevention calculations for oil-filled transformers, he would be engaging in steel structure design and analysis, he would be immersing himself in all of the woefully tedious activities that years ago he had striven to escape. So what? Sharon replied. Did he think that she loved her job? *Nobody* loves their job. You get your satisfaction from your husband or your wife, you get it from your family, she reminded him. And one day, you'll get it from our children. Remember children?

Edgar slapped Marcus on the back. "How about another pitcher," he said. For an instant, he resembled the Edgar of Marcus's youth again, a lanky sixteen-year-old boy in black soccer trunks and a yellow jersey.

"I'm not averse to having fun," Marcus said, and forced a smile. He was trying again for levity and good cheer, burdened by the weight of all the gloom he seemed incapable of shedding. He was painfully aware of his sobriety and languor, and of the guest's obligation to amuse and please his host.

"Hold on. Are you talking about meeting girls?" Edgar said.

"Oh God," Marcus said.

"Because if that's what you're talking about, there's not a lot of single women around. It's a family-heavy community."

"No, I meant… I don't know what I was talking about."

"Downtown, there's some bars where we can meet women. I'm not promising anything. But there's some places."

"I don't know."

"That's not a no."

"I'm only saying."

"You're not saying anything," Edgar upended his pint glass and drained what remained. "Why not?" he said, reaching for his thick barn jacket. "You had the right idea. Are we men or what?"

Harriet and MaryAnne were not the most beautiful women in attendance that evening at Jack's Black Smile, the boxy, noisy, brick-walled bar on Wallaby street, but they were certainly the kindest, since unlike the other women with whom Edgar attempted a conversation, Harriet and MaryAnne did not immediately walk away. As Edgar teased out their names and drink preferences, Marcus looked on with unexpected admiration for his friend. In high school, Edgar had possessed the self-assurance and charm of a lint catcher. At least some of the changes of the last fifteen years had been for the better.

"Let's see. Rum and Coke for MaryAnne and a Coors Light for Harriet," Edgar said.

"Other way around," Harriet said. She was a tall woman in her mid-thirties, with broad shoulders and a perky upright blonde ponytail. When she smiled her large pink gums flashed with the delighted overexposure of an exhibitionist. Harriet laughed loudly and happily, though not easily. In this, she expertly walked the line; she was neither too discerning to be unkind nor too lenient to be unsatisfying. When Marcus learned that she was an elementary school teacher, he felt a pang of envy for Harriet's students who—besides having their entire lives ahead of them—also had this friendly, robust woman to model their desires after.

"I like women with men's names. I think it's endearing," Edgar said, handing the tumbler with its plump quarter-lime garnish to Harriet.

"It's not a man's name," MaryAnne said.

"Harry," Edgar said.

"No one calls her Harry," MaryAnne said. Her features were small and dark, her eyes owlishly hooded, and the sight of her thin lips on the bottle made Marcus think, inexplicably, of a plug of black licorice.

"Marcus, did you know that MaryAnne is a stewardess? Maybe you were on the same flight," Edgar said.

"Flight attendant," MaryAnne said.

"Marcus flew in from San Jose this afternoon. Is that where you came from?"

"I came from Dallas."

"That would have been a crazy coincidence," Edgar said.

"Crazy," MaryAnne said, and pulled on her beer.

"Do you still like flying? After all this time? I think I'd lose interest," Edgar said.

"She hates it," Harriet volunteered.

"I like flying fine," MaryAnne said. "It's the passengers I could do without."

"They can be pretty bad, huh?" Edgar said.

"Tell them about the woman who put her baby up in the overhead bin. Her baby!" Harriet shrieked, laughing.

"She didn't know any better," MaryAnne said. "It was her first time on an airplane."

"Who's never been on an airplane?" Edgar said, shaking his head. "What else? You must have a ton of stories."

MaryAnne didn't reply. Marcus could feel her apathy; it was as prominent and visceral as rage, and though long ago he would have moved toward the bright sunlit delight of Harriet, after all that had happened to him recently, he felt a kinship to the obscure, ensnared dimness of MaryAnne. For the first time since arriving at the bar, he spoke.

"What's the worst thing you've ever done to a passenger?"

She turned to look at him. Whether gauging his seriousness or simply registering his presence, Marcus couldn't tell.

"There has to be something," he said.

"I'm not the vengeful type."

"You put sour milk in that guy's cof-fee," Harriet sang.

"Right. Something like that," MaryAnne said. "Sour milk."

Edgar laughed and pulled Harriet toward the jukebox.

"Come on. Help me pick some songs. If I have to listen to 'I Heard It Through the Grapevine' one more time I'll burn this place down."

"And what's the worst thing a passenger ever did to you?" Marcus said. He could see Edgar and Harriet negotiating the crowd toward the glass and metal stump of the jukebox and then, upon reaching it, their bodies converging to address it.

"I don't know," MaryAnne said.

"There has to be something."

"I don't remember."

"You're saying no passenger ever did anything bad to you," Marcus said.

"No. I'm saying I don't remember what the worst thing is."

"How is that possible?" Marcus said. He had come to believe that the worst fault was the one thing we always remembered, and confronted with this discrepancy he didn't know whether to be grateful or skeptical. He motioned to the bartender. The chalkboard posted a drink special, a beer and a shot for five dollars, and he ordered two. "So. How do you know Harriet?"

"Look, I appreciate the effort," MaryAnne said, rolling the new silver bottle between her palms, "but you don't have to do this."

"Do what?"

"I understand. You're playing wingman for your friend. Well I don't need to be distracted. I'm capable of entertaining myself."

"I'm not trying to distract you," Marcus said.

"Right. Of course not." She downed the shot then raised the bottle of beer to the sweet black stain of her lips. After a while she stopped and wiped her mouth with the back of her hand. "You find me deeply, deeply interesting," she said.

"Hey, I don't know what I said that offended you, MaryAnne—"

"That's it, use my name, it's more sincere."

"—but you seem to be having a conversation that I'm not having."

"I'm sorry," she said. "You're a good guy. Okay? You're a great guy. The world is full of great guys." She tapped him on the arm, once, twice, and then walked away.

"Marcus!" Edgar roared. He bullied his way through the crowd, his right shoulder rolled backwards, elbow flung out to ensure Harriet safe passage. They were both grinning and laughing and Marcus felt an instinctual forewarning of exclusion.

"We have to get out of here!" Harriet giggled.

"It's a *vampire* bar," Edgar whispered.

"Don't say it so loud! They'll hear you!" Harriet said.

There were indeed very different kinds of being drunk, Marcus thought.

"Come on," Edgar said, pushing his keys into Marcus's hand. "You're driving."

"At first, I thought it was a *pirate* bar..." Harriet said, while Marcus followed the pair out of the murky back room and across the main floor. The crowd had since thinned out—it was nearly closing time—and the patrons who remained had the weary steel of local unhappiness in their eyes. In the corner, an old man was swaying back and forth in what only the most bighearted euphemist would describe as dancing.

"*We're...almost...safe...*" Harriet whispered, as they pushed their way out into the cold North Carolina night. There was no moon in the sky, and in its absence the small stars flourished.

Marcus unlocked both doors and the three of them clambered into the cab of the truck, with Harriet squeezed in the middle. He switched on the ignition. The heater kicked in immediately, and Harriet, shivering, cranked the dial to maximum, but the engine was still cold and only sobering icy air raced out of the vents. Harriet huffed and squeaked at the assault while Edgar reached around and rubbed her shoulders.

"Where do I go?" Marcus said, setting the transmission to drive.

"Right out of the lot and then straight until the second light," Edgar said. "Then left."

"Don't listen to *him*! He doesn't know where I live."

"We're going to my house," Edgar said. "Marcus, tell her it's a nice house."

Harriet shook her head. Her blonde topknot waved like a palm tree. "I have to get up for class tomorrow."

"It's still early," Edgar said. "It's not even midnight."

"47 Allen Street," Harriet said to Marcus. "Right off of State Street. That's this big one here."

"Marcus, come on, tell her it's early."

Backing out of the lot, Marcus glanced in the rear view mirror and saw two men in duffel coats exit the bar. He tapped the brakes.

"What happened to MaryAnne?" he said.

"As a firefighter, I think I deserve a little more civic appreciation than this," Edgar said.

"You're not a firefighter!" Harriet said. She turned to Marcus. "Wait, is he a firefighter?"

"I'm joining the volunteer fire department. The last guy died and now there's finally a space," Edgar said.

"Oh that's terrible," Harriet said. "Was it a bad fire?"

"Boating accident," Edgar said.

"Does she need a ride? Is she still inside?" Marcus said.

Harriet shrugged. "She took my car a while ago."

Marcus released the brakes and they lumbered onto State Street. Despite Harriet's absent-minded directions, it didn't take long to reach the apartment building on 47 Allen Street. Marcus pulled up to the sidewalk.

"I can't find my keys," Harriet said, pawing through her leather purse. It was large and dark and soft, and in the dim light of the truck's cab it looked like a freshly excised organ of indeterminate use.

"Guess we'll have to go to my house after all," Edgar said.

After determining that she had given her house keys to MaryAnne along with her car keys, Harriet asked Edgar to call her and find out where she had gone. But Edgar explained that his cell phone, like Harriet's, had also died, and hadn't they ought to just get going? She could get her keys back tomorrow.

"Then Marcus can call," Harriet said, and rattled off seven digits that he dutifully plugged into his keypad while Edgar glared at him.

"Sorry to bother you," Marcus said, after MaryAnne had answered. "We're outside the apartment with Harriet and she can't get in. I know it's late."

"Which one are you?" MaryAnne said. "Chatty Cathy or Moody From San Jose?"

"Marcus. We were talking right before you left."

"I'm at the diner on the corner of Allen and Primary. It looks closed but it's open."

MaryAnne was seated in a booth by the window. Her narrow chin rested on the palm of her right hand as she read a plastic-sheeted library book.

Marcus sat across from her. "Sorry to interrupt your night," he said.

"Where's the happy couple," she asked, sliding the book beneath her plate and looking up.

"In the lobby of Harriet's building. The main entrance was propped open."

"Right."

"That's the worst thing about reading in restaurants," Marcus said, gesturing to her book, half-pinned beneath a messy dinner plate. "You have to leave food on the plate or they'll keep trying to take the plate away."

"They try anyway," she said, and reached into her purse. The sound of her hand rustling among the unknown trivia of her life grew noisier; it moved from the scuffle of rodents in the hedges to the rowdy brawl of a schoolyard wrestling match. She searched and searched but found nothing. Her lips tightened. The ends of her thin dark eyebrows turned down. Finally, she upended the contents of her purse onto the table with a clatter and, gritting her teeth, picked through the beautifying debris.

"I'm really sorry to bother you with this," Marcus said. "They're not even for me."

"I knew you were married," she said, plucking a slim set of keys out from beneath a jumble of black hair ties.

"I'm not married," Marcus said.

"Single men don't apologize."

"We're separated," he said.

Then, after a moment, he added, "Divorcing."

Her shoulders softened, and the corners of her eyes crinkled, and he felt the temptation of comfort, attention, and kindness as strongly and ruinously as he ever had.

"Any kids?" she said.

"One. A boy. Fourteen weeks old."

"That's hard," she said. Her voice had changed. It had retreated from the clipped remoteness of her lips to the warm rounded husk of her throat.

"Hardest year of my life."

"I mean hard for the boy," she said.

"Oh."

She gazed at the disarray on the table, but made no motion to gather it. "It's hard for you too, I'm sure."

As her sympathy washed over him, Marcus felt an exhilarating surge of relief. But then, like the foamy crest of a collapsing wave, shame and failure came crashing down after it.

"It was my fault," Marcus said. "I let her down—*us* down. I betrayed what we had." It didn't sound like him and MaryAnne seemed to notice, tilting her head slightly at the discordance. It was, Marcus understood, his wife's voice she was hearing. Since the recent cessation of Sharon's indictments and accusations, Marcus had come to provide them himself. He had listened to her litany of his offenses so many times that all he had to do was open his mouth and they would come pouring out, perfectly replicated.

"I don't need to hear about it," MaryAnne said.

"I don't like to talk about it," Marcus said. "Every day I just want to get further away from it. I don't know why I brought it up."

MaryAnne uncrossed her arms. "Well," she said, eyeing him, "you do have the look."

"What's the look?"

"The same one my cheating ex-husband had."

"Remorseful?"

"Male."

She laughed darkly, pushing aside the oval dinner plate. "That's not entirely fair. I know women who have stepped out on their husbands. A year after I married George I almost did it myself."

"What happened?" Marcus said.

She shrugged. "George was gone all the time. He's a pilot. I was still waiting tables. We almost never saw each other. It was like a long distance relationship only we lived together." She placed her middle finger on top of a loose nickel and made a counterclockwise circle with it. "Angus was one of my customers. He was half-British— he had this funny partial accent, everyone thought he was faking it, but it was really the way he talked. His a's turned into r's. Bananer. Idear." She reversed the nickel's direction. Thomas Jefferson's silver wig peeked out from below her nail bed. "He invited me out to drinks one night after work and I said yes, I don't know why, I guess I was flattered. We ended up at his apartment. Not much happened. Something, but not much. I felt terrible about it either way. When George finally got back I confessed everything. Threw myself at his feet." She dragged the nickel to the edge of the table and popped it upright with the base of her thumb. "George surprised me. He comforted me. Reassured me that we would be okay. It was…. I felt like I'd found the right man. You know? Here was proof. *He* was comforting *me*. What goodness I'd discovered, I told myself in awe. What bigness of spirit." She released the nickel and pressed its face back into the shellacked table. "Turns out he was already cheating on me. He'd slept with twenty, maybe thirty other women by then. Many of them would become my co-workers when I joined the airline." She smiled. "*Friends.*"

"I'm sorry," Marcus said.

"Yeah. Well."

"Did he regret it?"

"Allegedly."

"You didn't believe him."

"Why should I?"

Marcus shrugged. "Because he said it."

"Really? That's what I should have gone on in the face of all the evidence? Because he *said* it?"

"It's possible."

"Sure, it's possible. But is it likely?"

"You're beginning to remind me of my wife," Marcus said, and smiled. "Winning an argument with her was..." He was trying for lightheartedness but it backfired. MaryAnne narrowed her hooded eyes at him.

"This is how they started, isn't it," she said.

"I'm not sure I know what you mean," he said, although of course he did.

"The affairs started like this. With well-meaning, playful conversation in a restaurant. Or a bar. Or the galley or the hotel lobby or who knows where. Two adults airing their grievances about their spouses."

"We're just talking," Marcus said.

"Some people use candor for seduction." She looked out the window, at the black Carolina night. A sedan drove past with a dent in its side, low, just above the front tire.

"Why did you give up on your marriage?" Mary-Anne said.

"I didn't."

"Your wife kicked you out with a new baby? I find that scenario hard to believe."

"She couldn't forgive me."

"Why? Did you do it again or something?"

"No."

"Did you hit her?"

"God, no."

"She met someone else."

"I don't think so."

"It doesn't add up," MaryAnne said. "It's hard to be a single mom. She must have had some reason."

Marcus exhaled. "I had the affair while she was pregnant," he said.

MaryAnne didn't reply. Marcus tried to speak, to rupture the awful silence, but he could only stammer. "I didn't…"

"Didn't *what?*" The warmth in MaryAnne's voice had leached out, replaced by a cool brittleness.

Marcus had never been able to express the hopelessness and desperation he had felt prior to the affair without being accused by Sharon of attempting to excuse himself, and faced now with MaryAnne's rapidly escalating derision, he panicked, declaring, "It only lasted three months."

"What's a trimester among friends?" She shook her head. "I'm impressed. George has some big shoes to fill; you almost pulled it off."

"It's more complicated than you think," he murmured.

"Hey, you two should think about becoming roommates. If you could combine your respective shit-heel talents…"

Marcus closed his eyes. He had stopped paying attention. He knew everything MaryAnne might say to him next; he had already heard, articulated with Sharon's precise, enraged inflection, every slight or slur or judgment that she could possibly levy. For almost a year, while begging for her forgiveness, he had endured his wife demanding of him, sometimes as often as four or five times a day, "How can you *dare* to call yourself a man? What kind of a man does what you do? What kind of a man treats his wife the way you've treated me?" Over and over, he had absorbed the abuse, wearied the accusations and the imprecations and the character assassinations, "You're not a man. You're a *shadow* of a man. You're a worm." Sitting still, either mute or quietly apologetic, he had waited it out while the fever took hold of her and her precarious hope fled and she tore into him with all of the impassioned, punishing rhetoric of the injured party. He was a coward, he was disgusting, he was morally bankrupt, weak, and pathetic, he was loathsome, repulsive, despicable, vile, disgraceful, sleazy, disreputable, and filthy. Her contempt for him in these moments was exceeded only by her sadness, and when she would finally stagger out of her anger, jarred sideways from her wrath to reveal the pain beneath it all, he would find it nearly unbearable. Holding the slight shaking weight of her in the desperate hull of his arms, he would ask of himself the same damning questions that she had— and come up with the same absence of answers. What *had* he been thinking? How *could* he have thought it was possible to live two lives? What kind of a man *was* he? Yet despite his wife's enraged insistence to the contrary, he *hadn't* meant to hurt her. He had struggled and suppressed and denied and gamely smiled through so much that maddened him during the eight years they had been together in an attempt to avoid inflicting *precisely* this kind of pain and inciting this kind of fury. Put it off, sidestep it, let it go, he had reasoned again and again. Why fight her? Why argue? She wants what she wants and she's going to get it. You can't win with her. Stop trying. And if that failed to persuade him, he would recall the nuptial advice offered by his uncle David, married for thirty-two years, "Keep your mouth shut. Do you want to be right or do you want to be happy?" Only now, Marcus was neither right nor happy. The affair had been a private consolation he had allowed himself, a personal and reckless reprieve from the weary dissatisfaction of his life, and it had turned into a public punishment that he could not seem to escape. Even here, on the outskirts of a town that he had never visited and to which he hoped to never return, it followed him.

"Just give me the keys," Marcus said. "I've had this conversation already. I've heard it a thousand times."

"Hold on. Are you indignant? Are you seriously *indignant*?"

"I spent the past year enduring this kind of abuse from my wife—"

"Oh you poor dear. How did you handle it?"

"—I don't need to hear it now from a stranger."

"No, of course not," MaryAnne said. "That's not what you go to strangers for. You go to strangers for comfort. You go to strangers for sympathy and understanding and approval. You go to strangers because your wife doesn't listen to you and no one really understands you and isn't it *so hard* being misunderstood."

He leaned forward and snatched the keys away from her.

"What's the matter?" MaryAnne said. "Am I not bestowing upon you the forgiveness that you so richly deserve?"

Marcus entered the lobby of 47 Allen Street and called out for Edgar. Although he knew, intuitively, that the room was empty, he searched the lobby anyway, peering over the back of the cigarette-burnt couch, rotating the half dozen naugahyde-lined chairs to face him, even investigating the bank of bronze and glass-plated mailboxes where he had no hope of finding anyone, let alone a friend. It was past midnight. He was shaken and tired and though spending the night in Edgar's unused guest room didn't appeal to him much, at that moment Marcus was desperate to banish the unkind conspiracy of memory and regret that of late had overshadowed him, and he needed a bed to do this.

He got Harriet's apartment number from the thin metallic tag attached to her keys and rode the elevator to the fifth floor. Knocking softly on the door of apartment 5G, he waited for an answer. None came. He could see a flickering blue light coming from underneath the door, dimming and brightening with some unknowable pattern of intent. He knocked again, louder, but he was self-conscious about the time of night and feeling discouraged and frustrated by all that had occurred that evening and before he could stop himself he had slid the key into the lock and shouldered the door open.

The front door led directly into a compact white-tiled kitchen that had the look of casual disuse with which Marcus had once been intimately familiar when young and single and now, older and single again, he had become all too reacquainted. He didn't need to look inside the refrigerator to know what he would find: a quart of 2% milk, a bag of baby carrots, a wedge of orange cheese, and a shrunken, puckered lemon. Hurrying past the flimsy particle-board cabinetry, he followed the muffled sound of conversation into the living room, quietly calling out Harriet's name.

"She's asleep," Edgar said.

He was slumped on the couch, his back to Marcus, his socked feet resting beside a bottle of Jack Daniels on the glass coffee table. He had flung his huge barn jacket onto the floor and for a brief moment, locked in voluminous shadows with its brown sleeves crossed near the cuffs, it resembled the body of an animal.

"What are you doing?" Marcus said.

"Watching TV," Edgar said. On the blue screen, a Bobby Orr highlight reel was playing.

"I mean here," Marcus said. "If she's asleep, why are you here?"

"Do you think you're dangerous?" Edgar said.

"What?" Marcus picked up Edgar's jacket and stuffed it under his arm. "Let's go. We shouldn't be here."

"I was never dangerous when I was young." Edgar nodded slightly sideways at Marcus, the muscles of his neck slack. "We weren't raised like that. We were raised to be polite. Respectful. Thoughtful…. I lost a lot of girls that way. Because women," Edgar said, "they like dangerous men. The whole world knows that."

"Do you need me to help you up?" Marcus said.

"I can get up," Edgar said. He tried to rise but lost his balance and fell back onto the couch. He tried again, another tumble. Marcus offered his arm but Edgar just glared at it. On the third try, he righted himself, and though swaying, managed to circumnavigate the perilous glass table.

"That's what the female fascination with vampires is about, you know. Because they're *dangerous*."

"Oh yeah, of course," Marcus said. He wanted to get them out of the apartment before MaryAnne returned, and if that meant placating Edgar with a ridiculous conversation about the erotic appeal of vampires, so be it. "Dominance and submission," Marcus said, and crouched in front of the flat-screen TV. He ran his hand along the smooth black base in search of the power button.

"No, no, that's the mistake people make. It's not a metaphor for *sex*," Edgar said, shaking his head. "They're predators. They take their prey by the neck and drain them. They're hunters."

Finally, Marcus located the button. He pressed it with his index finger and the light and sound vanished from Harriet's living room.

"And women love it," Marcus heard the shadow that had replaced Edgar say. "Women love to be hunted. Or at least, they're supposed to."

Marcus paused. Without a word, he led Edgar through the kitchen and out into the hallway of the building. He unlocked the front door from the inside and left the key on the microwave before exiting the apartment. Then he faced his friend, blinking into the grim overhead fluorescence, and asked, "Did something happen while I was gone?"

Edgar stuck his hands in his pockets and made a fat, squelching sound with his lips, a grotesque noise somewhere between a chuckle and a sigh.

"Edgar, what happened?"

They arrived at Edgar's house at half past one in the morning and climbed out of the cab of the truck in weary tandem. They hadn't spoken at all during the twenty-minute drive and so Marcus was caught by surprise when, upon entering the kitchen and pouring himself a glass of filtered water, Edgar turned to him and said, "Nothing happened." He pulled a bottle of Tylenol out of a drawer and shook two red-striped tablets into his palm. "It's always the same thing," he said, swallowing the medicine. "Greeting, intrigue, consideration, disappointment, departure. Only the duration changes."

Marcus nodded. He was too distracted by his sense of relief, and too embarrassed by the disloyal and wanton unkindness of his imagination earlier that evening, to attempt an interpretation of Edgar's ramblings.

"Forget about tonight," Marcus said. "It's a Thursday. Never a good idea to go out on a Thursday."

"Tomorrow we go to bed early," Edgar said.

"Definitely. Even better idea."

"Sack out at eight and up by four..."

"Right."

"...And by six we're bagging our first deer."

"Absolutely," Marcus said. While living with Sharon, he had perfected the technique of automatic approval, agreeing without listening, and just as it had failed him then, it failed him now.

"Wait," Marcus called out to Edgar's retreating figure. "Bagging what?"

"I'm taking you deer-hunting Saturday morning," Edgar said.

"But I'm not a hunter. I've never been hunting before."

Edgar paused at the top of the stairs. His hand lingered along the smooth wooden throat of the banister.

"I'll teach you," he said.

"But..." Marcus began. He trailed off. All he had to say was no. All he had to do was explain that he had no interest in killing anything and thank you very much

for the offer. He knew this situation only too well—
more precisely, he knew its erotic analog—and there
was, indeed, a simple way out. But simple didn't mean
easy. Or, for that matter, true.

"I'll see you in the morning," Edgar said, and continued
on to his room.

But when Marcus awoke the next day, Edgar was
nowhere to be seen. Alone, Marcus padded around the
large empty house, the soles of his bare feet unpeeling
from the parquet floor. The previous evening was a
blurry collage of missteps and embarrassments and it
wasn't until noon had come and Marcus had camped
out on the screened-in porch with a red checkered
blanket tucked around his legs that he saw the family
of deer step lightly across the yard and he recalled
agreeing to the hunt.

Why had he agreed now, he asked himself, whereas
he'd never agreed before? His father-in-law was an avid
hunter and Marcus had declined his invitations without
hesitation. Deer, rabbit, partridge, quail, turkey—Marcus
had turned them all down in those first few years of
courtship and marriage. "I don't like to kill things," he
had said, by way of apology. But that wasn't really it;
his alleged pacifism, his righteousness, they weren't the
whole story. Marcus rejected Sharon's father because
the invitations were insincere, and correspondingly,

because Marcus's father-in-law *expected* him to decline. He didn't want Marcus coming along. Even when seemingly in defiance, Marcus marveled, he was submitting to someone's will.

He tore open the box of granola bars he'd brought along to the porch and removed one from its foil wrapper. Dunking it into the coffee mug, he let the sugar dissolve partially before placing the brown bar between his teeth. It was sweet and sticky and it tasted like four hundred calories of regret. He heard Sharon's voice instructing him in the failure of his latest decision. From the moment that they had gotten married, she had seen it as her duty to instruct him on wise choices. She loved him, so she would tell him how to be better. It was an elegantly simple thesis, and for eight years it ran head-on into the flawed antithesis that was Marcus himself. I should be eating an apple, he thought, as he stuffed a second granola bar into his mouth and pre-soaked a third. I should be cooking egg whites, or cutting up a fruit salad, or straining yogurt with muesli. I should be waking up earlier, drinking green tea, taking cold showers, getting some exercise. I should be looking for a new job. I should be updating my resume and writing emails to old co-workers. I should be doing something *else*. Or doing more of something, or doing less, or planning better or more efficiently or more forward-thinking. I should be trying harder. I should be more enthusiastic. I should be more animated and optimistic. I should be more forceful. I should be more confident. I should do and say and think and feel and know and understand and consider and encompass and validate and arouse and impress and prove, again and again, how good I can be.

The third granola bar broke in half while submerged and he had to fish around the mug with his whole hand, slopping warm coffee onto the blanket and his thighs, before managing to retrieve the soggy clump. He stuffed it into his mouth with satisfaction, but then proceeded to experience no pleasure. Had he learned anything? Marcus asked himself. He had internalized everything, but had he learned anything?

Chewing grimly, Marcus thought about the woman who had made the same mistake as Sharon had, which was to believe in him. *Alice*. He could not even recall her name without a reflexive spasm of fear, so conditioned by Sharon's explosions upon any mention of her. But there had been a time, not so long ago, when he could think of nothing but Alice. When they met at the office, Marcus had been charmed by her lightness and exuberance; she seemed unfettered by the worries and unhappiness that plagued him both at work and at home, the emerging anxiety that he was living someone else's life. Around Alice, Marcus felt giddy and reckless and resurgent.

Routinely inventing excuses to visit her, Marcus would linger by her desk as he tried everything he could to entertain her. He found in her dedicated attention a thrilling and long-absent sense of himself as a success. It was a strange and bewildering irony that he felt most authentic when in the midst of a performance, and it was perhaps because of this contradiction that he was not wholly surprised when they began sleeping together and he discovered that Alice was full of neither lightness nor exuberance. Happiness had been *her* performance, and with each successive tryst, she revealed more of her heaviness and sadness. Five months earlier, she had moved to San Jose to be close to her mother, who was suffering from Alzheimer's, and rather than rent an apartment, she lived with her older brother and his wife, contributing most of her meager salary as an administrative assistant to help defray her mother's medical costs. At twenty-eight, Alice felt too old to be slinking around her brother's house, and this sense of infantilism was only intensified by witnessing the slow disintegration of her mother, who seemed, in her cognitive distress, to be reverting to the incapability of a toddler. Alice would tell Marcus about helping to dress her mother—fastening her diaper, reminding her that pajamas are worn in the evening—and in these mundane and discouraging descriptions he heard none of the saccharine affirmation provided by movies or TV shows but the agitated disbelief of a woman encountering personalized tragedy on a daily basis. There was much to flee at home, and with Marcus's help, Alice gladly fled it.

Did he love Alice? It was a question Marcus would face down again and again once the affair had been revealed, and his confused and itinerant answers early on failed to reassure Sharon. Try as he might, he could never quite articulate what he had felt for Alice, the curious intensity of what they had shared; it had been both a diversion and a coming together, a kind of eroticized melancholy. The only thing that would satisfy Sharon was an absolute denial, however, and she took Marcus's honest yet byzantine replies as cowardly confirmation that he had fallen in love with another woman. Marcus could not have chosen a less tactful moment in his life to embrace the messy contradictions and incriminations of the human heart; his wavering ensured that he antagonized not only his wife but Alice's brother, who persuaded Alice to sue the company for sexual harassment (the case quickly settled out of court by Sharon's father). They needed the money for their mother, Alice apologized to Marcus later, in a text message that he would never return.

Marcus glanced up at the cry of a bird. In the yard, the family of deer had lost interest and was moving on. Five bodies leaped over the fence with the divine effortlessness of sin.

He had hurt her too. Staying with Sharon until the baby was born, trying to make the marriage work, he had broken Alice's heart. In the end, he had hurt everyone.

That was his life now, he reasoned. Hurting things.

So be it.

He aimed an invisible rifle at the smallest of the deer as it bounded for the horizon and, closing one eye, he pretended to fire.

"Short and light, with a handy bolt action and a nice accurate carbine," Edgar said, lifting the rifle out of the black and silver steel-plated gun safe. "Six and a half pounds and a 243 Win for the cartridge—fine killing power and the recoil is manageable. She's a good start for you," he said, handing the rifle to Marcus.

Marcus took hold of the stock with one hand and let the barrel swing down and smack against the palm of his other hand. "It's smaller than I expected," he said.

"The barrel's only twenty inches. But in the brush you're going to want that maneuverability. You won't be taking any shots longer than 200 yards... there's also the Ruger," Edgar said brightly. He pulled out a second rifle and swapped with Marcus. "The barrel's even shorter but she's about half a pound heavier. Trim and deadly. Controlled feed. Fast handling. Old-school adjustable iron sight."

"I don't know. Whichever you think."

"Six of one," Edgar said. "You can't go wrong."

"I'll take the first one," Marcus said.

"You know when it's a fit. It feels good, right?
In your arms."

Edgar retrieved the Ruger and delicately placed both
rifles back into the safe. "I used an old Remington 788
bolt action when I first started hunting. Thought I was
upgrading by getting rid of it. Wish I still had it."

He switched off the garage light and climbed the stairs
that led back into the house. Marcus followed a few feet
behind, uneasy and indolent. He had spent the entire
day in a slept-in gray tee shirt and jeans without the
slightest consideration but now, confronted by Edgar,
whose tailored navy blue suit projected the achievement,
respectability, and decorum that Sharon had so vocally
and vociferously desired for Marcus, he felt embarrassed.

"Does it ever seem unfair to you?" Marcus said.

"Unfair?"

Marcus hesitated. He didn't know quite what he was
asking, about which of the hundred thousand inequities
that populate the world and merit inquiry.

"Hunters keep the deer population in check. We're
like wolves or cougars," Edgar said. He pulled a six-pack
out of the fridge and untangled two cans of beer from
the extruded plastic coil. He threw one to Marcus, who

caught the cold red bullet against his chest. "Fairness is a human invention."

They ordered dinner and watched the second half of a basketball game on the enormous flat screen until it arrived. Edgar paid the delivery boy while Marcus set the table, then they both unpacked the bags, arranging the little white boxes with such swiftness, symmetry, and accord that the act looked choreographed. As they moved around each other, Marcus felt the first real and unequivocal affection for Edgar since coming to visit.

"I meant to tell you before—thanks for putting me up. It's a great house," he said, although in fact he had little love for the drafty, oversized building. But he had long since learned to substitute the indirect praise of objects for direct sentiment when expressing affection with men. He did it without even being aware of it, and now, believing the substitution to be the true sentiment, Marcus defended the house when Edgar told him that he intended to sell it once the market turned around.

"You don't just give up a place like this. With that yard, and animals coming into it to visit?"

"It's a family house," Edgar said. "Do you see a family?"

He cracked open another beer and poured it into a souvenir pint glass. It occurred to Marcus that Edgar was drunk. His eyes looked unfocused and the muscles of his jaw seemed to be moving independently of language or meaning.

"Things change," Marcus said.

Edgar rubbed the disintegrating gold decal with his thumb. He brought the glass to his lips. "You should think about moving out here. We could be neighbors again."

Marcus nodded. They hadn't really been neighbors, but Marcus did not want to correct Edgar.

"You could crash with me until you found a job," Edgar said. "I've got nothing but space."

"Yeah, I don't think—"

"It'd be fun," Edgar said. "We have a lot of catching up to do."

Marcus used the edge of his fork to halve a blackened asparagus tip and, spearing it carefully, he placed it between his teeth.

"Hey, remember junior year French class?" Edgar said. "You had a crush on what's her name, the blonde who wore the big floppy sun hat at graduation. What was it? Karen? Kelly?"

"Carrie Fitzsimmons."

"Carrie! I knew you'd remember her name. You should look her up."

"Maybe."

Edgar took a mouthful of beer and swallowed. "Seriously, you should see what she's up to. Tell her we're going to be roommates. It'll crack her up."

Marcus glanced up at the softly illuminated boxes nested along the highest kitchen shelf. "Listen, it's a generous offer, letting me stay here, but I can't leave San Jose."

"Right. Because you're going to try harder," Edgar said. He shook his head with disgust. "It doesn't matter what you do. Haven't you figured that out yet? It isn't up to us. *They* decide." He stood and pushed himself free of the table. "When a woman is done with you, she's done with you forever."

Once, Marcus would have thought it a relief to be stripped of standards, to be divested of any code of conduct. All of the weight of expectation would lift clear off of his shoulders and he would be free, at last, to think and feel and act as he pleased. No more repression. No more concession. No more inhibition or restraint or pandering. Every action would possess, in the fearless intentionality of its execution, a purity that had heretofore been unmatched by all the emotional and behavioral compromise that love required. But lying in the guest bedroom that night, unable to sleep, Marcus again encountered the discouraging truth that the reality of a thing imagined was very different from the dream. Whereas once, in the swamp of his anxiety and unhappiness, he had longed for the release of freedom, what he felt now was not deliverance but loss.

He burrowed under the heavy white down cover, nestling his head among a heap of decorative pillows, and listened to the breath moving in his chest. Every system of meditation that he had tried in the past year to quiet the anxious mournful chatter of his mind had directed him to his breath. But as of yet, no amount of self-aware surveillance had distracted him even momentarily from his thoughts.

Eyes closed, he pictured Sharon with their son, a small pink stranger whose body was still so new that the simple act of raising his head constituted an impossible challenge. He wondered if and how she spoke of him to the boy, and whether one day the boy would want anything to do with him. Marcus had been unsure about having children. For this decision, too, he had submitted to the overwhelming force of Sharon's personality, whose longings and needs seemed inalienable rights, whereas Marcus's were merely whims. Before the boy had been born, while lost in the disarray of the affair, Marcus had consoled himself that boys naturally hewed to their mothers, and so any distance on Marcus's part would go unnoticed. But now that the boy was here, and Marcus was no longer trying to escape his life but rather secure it, he found the prospect of estrangement from the boy an unbearable cruelty.

Retrieving his cellphone from the bedside table, he propped himself up against the pillows and opened his photo folder. The images were chronologically sorted in descending order; the first to appear were from the hospital, just after the birth of his son. Tiny, with wide-set disconcerted eyes, the boy looked as red and pulpy as a skinned rabbit. Marcus swiped quickly among the photographs—in his excitement, he had taken dozens of nearly identical shots, and had yet to delete any of them—until he came across a photo of Sharon. She was lying in the hospital bed and holding the swaddled newborn to her chest while smiling wearily at the camera. Marcus expanded the image. Even under-lit and pixelated, her face looked happy. Despite their struggles leading up to the birth, Sharon had allowed him to be present during the delivery, and when the pain of the contractions had grown particularly fierce, she had reached for his hand. Crouching beside her, squeezing her hot, tense fingers with his own, he had attempted to reassure her. She looked at him, her mouth open, the muscles around her eyes taut with agony. It was terrifying and heart-breaking and he stopped whispering his senseless prayer that she would be okay and instead simply leaned into her, until slowly, he felt her shoulders relax, and her shallow breath deepen. Together, they continued like this, mutually engaged in the ordeal of her pain, and in

these long and agonizing moments Marcus felt closer
to his wife than he had in years. After nearly having
given up on their ever possessing intimacy again,
Marcus was astonished to discover it now returned to
them, brought back by the pain and the fear, by the
ache and the exhaustion and the obliterating sensation
of turning oneself inside out.

Except he hadn't possessed it. He had only held it for
a moment, like his son, cradled it with clumsy appreciation
then watched strangers wipe away the blood and take it
into another room into which he could not enter. Upon
returning home from the hospital, Sharon hired a sullen
Jamaican nanny to help with the baby, and in Marcus's
occasional visits, he experienced little, if any, of the tender-
ness that he had glimpsed at the hospital. There had
been one rapturous day when Sharon had lingered beside
him as he held the baby, and the lavender-vanilla smell
of her hair and the brush of her shoulder against his
had sent him into a treacherous spasm of hope. Here
was the girl with whom he had fallen in love so long ago,
the girl who would come over to his shabby apartment
and sit cross-legged on the couch and complain happily
about her day. He would console her eagerly, excitedly;
all he wanted to do was please her, charm her, distract
her, as she did so easily for him. But at the next visit,
and the one after that, Sharon did not linger beside

Marcus. Nor did she lean down, as she had when they first met, and let him remove her glasses and gently kiss the dark pink stripes that the frames had scored onto the sides of her nose. She simply handed Marcus the child and left. Afterwards, he walked around the living room in a daze, while the nanny took intermittent breaks from penciling among her word search puzzle to issue him glares more suitable for a murderer.

And it was from this bereaved, frustrated memory that Marcus's great revelation arrived. Tomorrow morning he would go on the hunt with Edgar, as planned, but after stalking a white-tailed deer and fixing the helpless creature in his sights, he would decide—suddenly, charitably—to let it live. He would lower the barrel of his rifle and shake his head, demonstrating with this tender act of restraint the noble forbearance of which he was still capable. And as the deer sprang off through the brushes, saved by Marcus's goodness from a premature death, Marcus too would be saved from a legacy of disgrace.

Having successfully orchestrated his long-delayed redemption, Marcus now found sleep impossible. On top of his anticipation, the sheer inactivity of his day intensified his insomnia. He tossed and turned for an hour, then got out of bed and rifled through the house for something to knock him out, but the medicine cabinets in all three bathrooms failed him. Faced with a restless night and a sleepless dawn, Marcus grabbed the keys from the bowl by the microwave and headed to the driveway.

It was a cold Carolina night, with air as thin and slight as a blade of grass. Marcus zipped up the borrowed down jacket and crossed the front lawn. Edgar's truck was missing—pre-loaded with hunting supplies and parked in the garage, Marcus now recalled—but the hatchback had been left at the top of the driveway. Marcus fished in the bowl for the keys to the hatchback and unlocked it with a press of a button. The car beeped in confirmation and its headlights flashed twice. Out of the corner of his eye Marcus caught movement, and he turned to see the family of deer standing alert on the hilly banks of the road. The animals were well lit by the moon, exposed yet curious, and as Marcus watched, more and more climbed out of the safety of the bushes until they were ten, then twelve, then fifteen in number. These suburban pests were not the deer they would be hunting, Edgar had told him during dinner, and staring back at them, Marcus felt affronted by the slightness of their status. To him, they looked as vital and untouchable as stars and, mounting and descending the hill, they formed a luminous constellation whose greater shape was shifting and magnificent and all too brief.

Marcus climbed into the car. He blew warm breath onto his hands and rubbed them together. After driving the truck, it felt strange, almost childish, to sit so low to the ground. He switched on the ignition and the headlights and, glancing over at where the passenger seat had once been, a black space resembling the torn-out socket of a molar, he set of for the nearest 24 hour convenience store. There was no traffic at that time of night, and he covered the eight miles in almost as many minutes.

A bell suspended above the door jingled when Marcus entered. Except for the cashier, the store was empty, though this did nothing to dim the bright disposable hope of all such stores, and whistling softly, Marcus navigated the aisles in search of medicine. He found a shelf loaded up with allergy relief, flu and cold remedies, gas tablets, vitamin packs, and some homeopathic pills, and after sifting among the boxes, checking ingredients and reading the instructions, he carried the three likeliest candidates to the register.

"Which of these is best for sleep?" Marcus asked the cashier.

The cashier was a tall and rangy man in his fifties with traces of acne on his cheeks. He removed his glasses from the front pocket of his shirt and placed them on the end of his nose. Taking his time, he held up each box individually for inspection.

"None of these is for sleep," he said finally. "Try whiskey."

"I can't be hung over. I'm going hunting tomorrow morning." Marcus picked the middle box and pushed aside the other two. The cashier rang up the price.

"First time hunting?" he said.

Marcus smiled.

"How did you know?"

He set off for the house in a fit of hopeful, fortified triumph. As before, there was no traffic, and the hatchback raced along this newest installment of night with neither rival nor friend in sight. The main road led to a secondary road and the secondary road to a back road and it was on this slim unlit back road, flanked by low-hanging chalk maples and eastern box elders and rough-skinned sweet birch, that Marcus felt the car shake and jump from the force of impact. He hit the brakes with haste but he could see the ruined blue hood in front of him, folded in on itself like a goodbye letter creased into thirds and slipped into an envelope, and he understood that something grave and irreparable had happened.

He shifted to park and turned off the radio. He activated the hazards and dimmed the heat and repositioned his seat and flipped down the visor and untangled the seat belt and performed every act of maintenance that he could think of before he had exhausted the activities that would keep him in the safety of the car and, subsequently, the past. Instinctively, he knew what he had just hit, but as long as he remained inside, he would not have to face it. He was tired of facing things. Hadn't he done enough of that lately? If he was destined to a lifetime of mistakes, could he not be permitted, at least, the slight mercy of ignorance?

Through the windshield, ten feet up the road, Marcus thought he glimpsed the body, and he quickly looked away. He located his cell phone lodged beside the accelerator and retrieved it. He pressed "Contacts" and then "Favorites" and found Sharon's name still there, at the top position, although it had been weeks since they had spoken. A software program inside the phone was supposed to recalibrate these rankings according to usage and frequency and duration and a host of other complex technical variables that seemed, in the end, to have been overwhelmed by the simple data points of heartbreak and regret. He thought, as he did every day, about calling her, but he couldn't bear now—especially not now— to hear the softness of her voice. It was not Sharon's unkindness that he feared anymore, but her kindness. Her kindness told him that she had let him go.

Marcus kept his gaze averted from the windshield and scrolled through his phone. At the top of his most recent calls he saw MaryAnne's number. In this new and violent upset, he did not think of MaryAnne's lack of sympathy, of her fluency with punishment, he thought only of this woman on the other end that would save him, and he pressed the small green icon initiating a call. On the fourth ring, the line clicked alive. Before he could stop himself, he said, "It's Marcus."

"Marcus," she repeated.

"I hit something. I didn't mean to!" He rubbed his face with his hand, digging his fingers into the bony ridge of his brow "What if I have to come back and shoot it?" he said. "What if it's not dead? I can't do that. I..."

He trailed off, glancing helplessly toward the windshield and beyond it, the dark promise of the night's revelation.

"I don't know how this happened," he murmured. "I don't know what to do."

He pressed the phone tighter to his ear, straining to hear a reply, but all that came back was the hushed sound of MaryAnne's breathing.

"I'm sorry," he said. "I'm sorry. I shouldn't have called you." He shook his head. "What do I do now?"

Still, she didn't answer him. But he could hear her on the end of the line, her breath rising and falling with quiet incidence. He felt the warm dampness of his own breath as he exhaled, matching hers, and the anxious beating of his heart beneath the muscle and bone of his chest: bereft, ragged, pursued.

He hung up.

Then he stepped out into the cold and circled around to see what he had done.

The deer lay in the middle of the road, facing away from the car as if in girlish rebuff. White markings periodically interrupted its toffee-colored coat—around its eyes, and above its mouth, and lining the inside of its ears. The feathery underside of its tail was also white and, for a moment, Marcus thought he saw the tail flick upwards. But when he looked again, more carefully, he realized that it was only his hope that had animated its tail, and no part of the animal had moved or would ever move again.

He leaned with his hands against the dented hood and closed his eyes.

When he reopened them he walked toward the deer without hurry, admiring the slenderness of its frame and the fineness of its small, white-limned mouth, and most of all, the candid gawkiness of its limbs as it rested, in death, from any further pursuit of grace. He walked toward it, thinking that he would take it into his straining arms; that he would carry it across the road and put it in the space next to his seat; that this was the thing left to do.

Acknowledgements

I would like to thank Deena Drewis, my visionary editor, for her invaluable insights. Thank you to Darcy Cosper, Tim Fitts, Matthew Freeman, Greg Henderson, Deborah Treisman, and Paul Wernick, who read an early version of the novella, and to Meredith Arthur, Kimberly Burns, Colin Dickerman, and Sara Mercurio, for weighing in on the question of titles. David Daley demonstrated unflagging enthusiasm, discernment, and friendship in nearly every aspect of the publication process. Adam Langer, Jim Lynch, Jean Nathan, and all those who showed their support, thank you for your kindness.

Most of all, I am indebted to my wife, Molly, whose encouragement, sensitivity, and passion for writing—this enduring and inconvenient mania—have proven essential to my happiness. As has she.